HAPPY
SAINT
PATRICK'S
DAY

Happy St PaTrex Day

This Book Belongs to

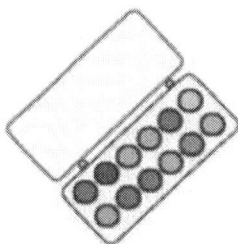

_____

_____

TEST YOUR COLOR

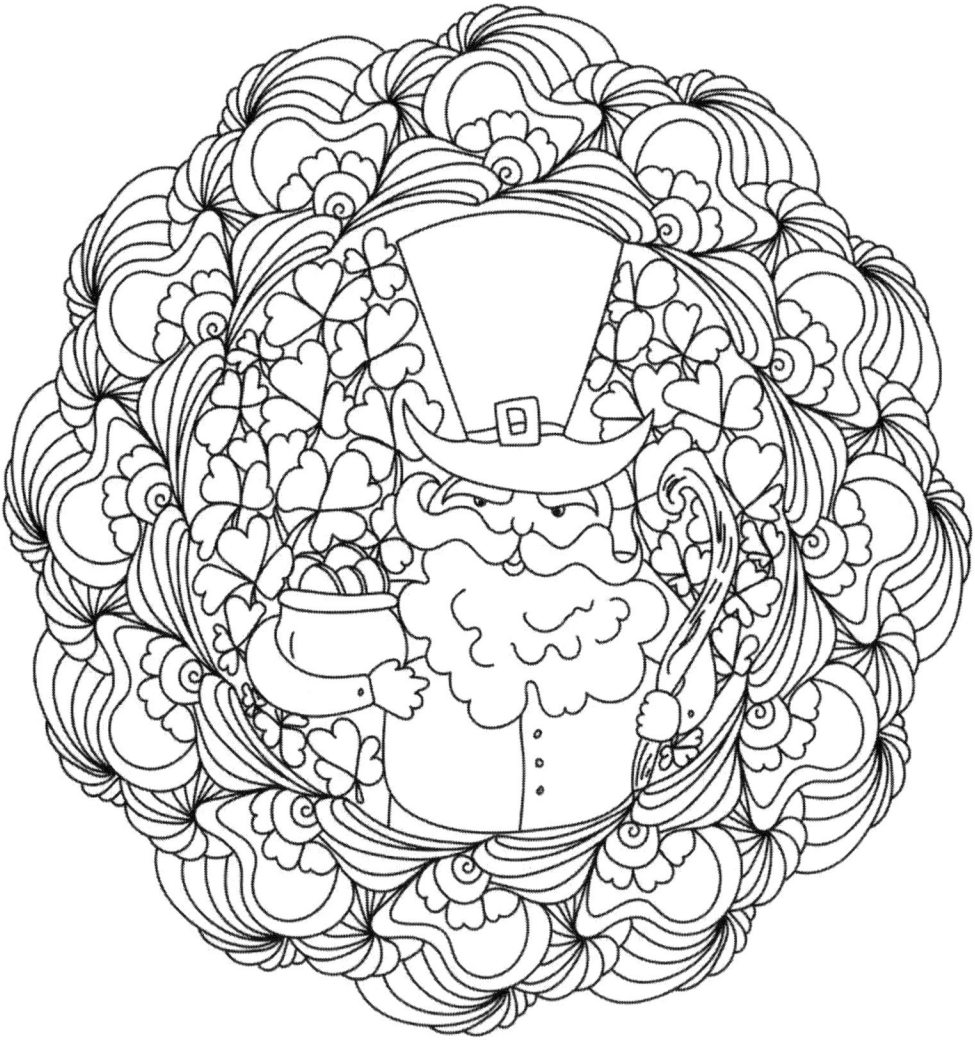

Happy St PaTrex Day

Tree of Life

Yes, I'm an IRISH GIRL I SPEAK FLUENT SARCASM

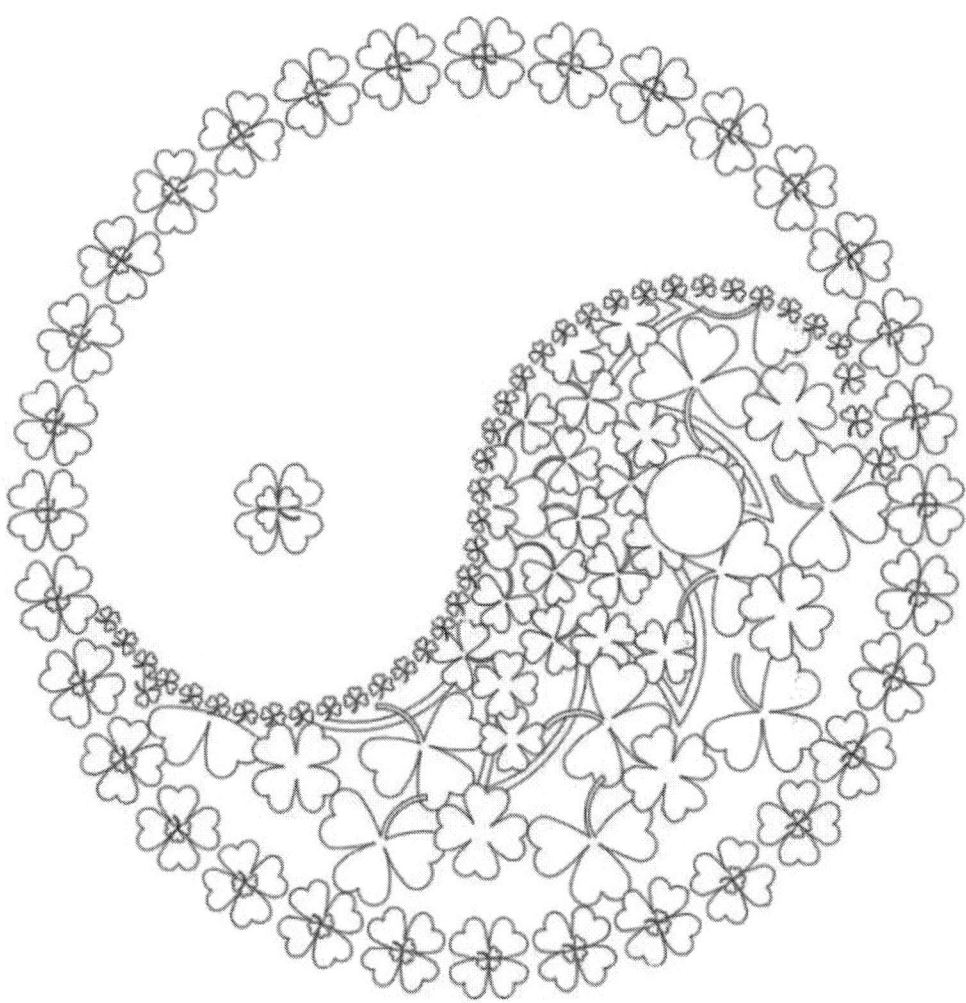

Happy
St. Patrick's
Day!

thank
you

Made in the USA
Las Vegas, NV
15 March 2022